Dobbs Ferry, New York

Dear Girls and Boys,

Sometimes it is nice to know if a book is about something that really happened. The pioneer girl in this book, Ann Hamilton, was a real person. Much of what happens to her here is just a story but some of it is true. The happy ending is true and as long as she lived, Ann told this part of the story to her children and her children's children. I know because Ann Hamilton was my great-great-grandmother.

There really was a David and a Daniel too, and a Mr. and Mrs. Hamilton, and a Cousin Margaret, and if you read to the end of this book, you'll find out what happened to them even after the story is over.

Hamilton Hill is known as Ginger Hill now, but grapevines still grow by the side of the road. The little church is really there just where David said it would be, and whenever I can, I go to church there.

Jean Fritz

Other Puffin Books by Jean Fritz

BRADY

THE DOUBLE LIFE
OF POCOHONTAS

EARLY THUNDER

STONEWALL

TRAITOR

THE CABIN FACED WEST

Jean Fritz

THE CABIN
FACED WEST

Illustrated by Feodor Rojankovsky

PUFFIN BOOKS

PUFFIN BOOKS
Published by the Penguin Group
Penguin Putnam Books for Young Readers,
345 Hudson Street, New York, New York 10014, U.S.A.
Penguin Books Ltd, 80 Strand, London WC2R ORL, England
Penguin Books Australia Ltd, Ringwood, Victoria, Australia
Penguin Books Canada Ltd, 10 Alcorn Avenue, Toronto, Ontario, Canada M4V 3B2
Penguin Books (N.Z.) Ltd, 182-190 Wairau Road, Auckland 10, New Zealand

Penguin Books Ltd, Registered Offices: Harmondsworth, Middlesex, England

First published by Coward-McCann, Inc., 1958
Published in Puffin Books 1987
40 39 38 37
Copyright © Jean Fritz, 1958
All rights reserved
Printed in the United States of America
Set in Caledonia

Library of Congress Cataloging in Publication Data
Fritz, Jean.   Cabin faced west.
Summary: Ten-year-old Ann overcomes loneliness and learns to appreciate
the importance of her role in settling the wilderness of western Pennsylvania.
1. Frontier and pioneer life—Pennsylvania—Fiction. 2. Pennsylvania—Fiction]
I. Title.   PZ7.F919Cab   1987   [Fic]   86-16918   ISBN 0-14-032256-6

Puffin Books ISBN 0-698-11936-3

TO MICHAEL

THE CABIN FACED WEST

Chapter One

Aɴɴ Hᴀᴍɪʟᴛᴏɴ swept the last of the day's dust out of the door into the sunset. Even the cabin faced west, Ann thought as she jerked the broom across the flat path the daylight made as it fell through the open doorway. It was the only place the daylight had a chance to come in. The cabin was solid logs all the way around without another opening anywhere. Its back was turned squarely against the East just as her father had turned his back. Just as her older brothers, David and Daniel, had.

"We've cast our lot with the West," her father had said as he stood in the doorway the day the cabin was completed. "And we won't look back."

That was the time Daniel and David had made the Rule. Ann supposed she must have been pouting because Daniel had looked straight at her when he had spoken.

"The first one who finds fault with the West," he had said in that important voice he used more than ever since he had passed his eighteenth birthday, "will get . . ."

He had hesitated a moment and David had finished the sentence. "Will get a bucket of cold spring water on top of his head." He had laughed as he pulled one of Ann's brown braids. David was only a year younger than Daniel but Ann couldn't imagine that he would ever sound as grown up. There was too much twinkle to David. Still, both the boys had taken the Rule seriously.

They were always trying to catch each other in a complaint and had discovered all kinds of ways to turn a sentence around at the last minute to mean something altogether different than it had started out to mean. Neither one had been caught yet.

As for Ann, she had made her mouth into a tight line when Daniel had started the Rule. She knew she had complained too much. All up and down the endless mountains to this lonely hill last spring, she had complained. But the day Daniel made the Rule she stopped. There was no use complaining now anyway. There didn't even seem to be much use talking. Her mother and father were always so busy, and the boys—well, you couldn't talk to boys.

That was another trouble. Every cabin from here to the nearest settlement was filled with nothing but boys and babies. There wasn't one girl anywhere near ten years old. Uncle John Hamilton and Aunt Mary who lived halfway down the hill on one side didn't have any children. And the new squatters who had just put up their makeshift shack at the bottom of the hill on the other side—what did they have? A boy, of course. He was eleven years old, but a boy all the same and, from what Ann had seen, he was the worst yet.

Ann sighed as she leaned the broom against the wall near the hearth where her mother was rocking the baby.

"Ann." Mrs. Hamilton looked up with a little frown between her eyes. "Ann, there's no more work for you today. I can finish alone. You run along, if you've a mind to."

Ann kneeled down on the floor beside her mother. She held a finger for the baby to catch but he wasn't interested. He was only ten weeks old, too little to do much but sleep and eat. But he was sweet—pink and soft and new-smelling.

"Howdy, little Johnny-cake," Ann whispered softly. Then suddenly she jumped up, dropped a kiss on the top of her mother's head and ran to the old stump David had sawed off for a stool. She dragged it over to the long log wall and, climbing on it, stood on her tiptoes. She reached above the row of pegs where the clothes were

hanging to the top log just under the sleeping loft. This log jutted out a bit and was wide enough, Ann had discovered, to hold the few dear possessions that in all the family belonged only to her. She ran her hand along the log. Yes, there were her blue Gettysburg shoes that she was saving for winter and special occasions. Only there didn't appear to be any special occasions here. Nothing was special enough even for her mother to use the linen tablecloth or the twelve china plates that were stored away.

Ann moved her fingers until she felt the piece of cloth she had wrapped around her two blue satin hair ribbons to keep them clean. Next on the shelf came Semanthie. Semanthie was the tiny doll her father had carved in Gettysburg when he had had time to do something with wood besides chop it down. Ann took Semanthie off the shelf and looked at her round face painted with black eyes and red lips that were fading. Maybe she would take Semanthie for a walk to the road. Semanthie never laughed or scolded when Ann found fault with things, the way her brothers did. Even when Ann sometimes cried a little because she was homesick for her cousin Margaret, for school, for the good times she had left behind her in Gettysburg—even then Semanthie just looked at her with those black, unblinking eyes and those pale, unmoving lips. No, Ann decided, she didn't want to take Semanthie with her tonight. She put her back on the shelf and instead took down a little brown book and her one precious pencil.

Ann handled the book gently, for this was truly her dearest possession. This was her diary. Cousin Margaret had given it to her when she had left Gettysburg—was it only five months ago? Ann had been sitting stuffed down into one side of a pack saddle with clothes piled on her lap and all around her when Margaret had run up with the brown book.

"Here," she had said, thrusting it into Ann's hands. "It's too late now for them to say there isn't room. It's a book for you to write in. There won't likely be any schools where you're going so you can practice your writing in this."

There wasn't even much paper where she had been going, Ann thought, and so she had written in small, small letters to make the book last longer. Somehow putting down on paper what she was thinking and doing made Ann feel better than any amount of talking to Semanthie. The words didn't seem to be so wasted. This way she could catch hold of them and make them stay.

"I'm glad you keep practicing your letters, Ann." Her mother smiled as she saw Ann take down the brown book. "Some day we'll have some books for you to read."

Some day. There they were again—those two words that Ann had learned to hate.

"And some day," her mother was going on, "your father will build you a proper shelf to put your things on."

Ann looked at her mother. Did "some day" satisfy her mother, she wondered, the way it did all the others? Ann couldn't tell. Her mother looked so tired with that little crease between her eyes even when she tried to talk hopeful.

Ann went over and gave her mother a quick hug before she started for the door. "I'm going down to the road," she said.

Then as Ann glanced over her shoulder, her eyes rested again on the long log wall hung with pegs.

"And some day," Ann added rather fiercely, "we are going to have windows cut in that wall."

"Yes," her mother agreed. "Maybe this winter when your father has more time."

Ann didn't hear. She was already out of the cabin and skipping through the clearing down to the road.

Chapter Two

OF ALL the places on her father's hill, Ann liked the road best. She had a feeling about the road. Sometimes her mother said she had a "feeling in her bones." She couldn't explain it; it was just there. That was the way Ann was about the road.

As she stood now, looking down where the road dropped over the hill and melted away under the great trees and tangled grapevines,

Ann felt the usual excitement. It was silly to feel that way, she told herself. Nothing ever happened at this end of the road; everything exciting was at the other end—the Gettysburg end. Certainly there was nothing exciting about the road itself. Ann shuddered when she remembered the long, weary miles the road took up each of those dreadful mountains and the slipping, sliding miles down the other sides. Yet when Ann was alone, she usually came right here. It was almost as if the road held some kind of special promise for her.

She scuffed at a pebble with her bare toes and laughed. "I must be getting wilderness fever," she said half aloud, "to be thinking like that."

All the same, Ann felt better as she walked over to her favorite sitting spot at the side of the road where a group of trees formed a cozy half circle at her back. She dropped down on the ground, smoothed out her yellow linsey skirt and opened her brown book. With her eyes half closed, she turned over in her mind what she wanted to write. Behind her she could hear the sounds that meant evening. Daniel was having trouble with the two cows. Ann could tell by the way he was urging them forward and by the stop-and-go sound of the cowbells. David must have brought the evening water up from the spring because Ann could hear him in front of the cabin calling to Daniel.

"Are you having a hard time with those cows, Daniel?"

Ann could picture David's twinkle as he tried to catch Daniel in a complaint. She could also picture very clearly indeed Daniel's scowl as he rumbled back his answer.

"These are the two most stub—" he began but then he stopped short. "These are the two most co-operating, obedient cows this side of the Alleghenies," he roared.

He hadn't been caught yet. Ann smiled to herself and turned to her diary.

"Today I worked in the vegetable garden," she wrote carefully in small, neat letters, "and I churned. I helped dip candles."

She read what she had written and shook her

head impatiently. It wasn't what she had meant to write at all. Quickly she added, "I am sitting by the road, which is very empty. I wish Margaret were here. Nothing ever happens." Ann was writing so fast now that her letters were beginning to go crooked down the page. "Nothing," she wrote again.

Just at that moment, however, something did happen. As she bent over her diary, Ann suddenly felt a strange tickling on the back of her neck. At the same time there was a rustling noise behind her. She sat very still. She didn't want to look around. Suppose it was one of those mad wolves that had been prowling the forest. Suppose it was one of the gang of horse thieves that had been causing trouble farther west in the county. Suppose it was an unfriendly Indian. There hadn't been any unfriendly Indians on the hill for a long time, but you could never tell. Something brushed across the top of Ann's head —across her *scalp*, she thought, and jerked her braids around to the front of her shoulders.

"Oo—oooooooh-oo," came the call of an owl in the tree above.

Ann shivered. Maybe it was an Indian imitating an owl.

She closed her book slowly and then, gathering her courage for one swift movement, she jumped to her feet and swung around to face whatever was there.

At first all Ann could see was a grapevine rope dangling from the tree. She followed the rope to where it disappeared in the tree and there, half hidden among the leaves, was the new squatter boy. One arm was swinging the grapevine rope gently to and fro and his face was peering over the branch in a teasing grin.

Ann put her hands on her hips. "Andy McPhale," she called, "just what do you think you're doing?"

"Playin'." Andy started swinging the rope in wider and wider circles until Ann had to jump back to keep from being hit.

Then he dropped the rope to the ground and jumped down after it.

"Scared ya, didn't I?" he asked. Andy grinned

with an impishness that for a moment made Ann think of David, but as she looked at him again she wondered how she could ever have thought of such a comparison. His dark hair was long and shaggy and as untouched-looking as forest undergrowth. He stood with his hands behind his back in a slouch as though his body wasn't used to going anywhere particular or having anything important to do.

As he stepped closer to Ann, he jerked his chin awkwardly in the direction of the book she was holding.

"I see you're eddicated," he said. "Where did you get your learnin'?"

Ann thought she caught a wishful look in Andy's eyes but she must have been mistaken. He was all mockery now.

"Back home," Ann answered. "I went to school back home in Gettysburg."

Andy squinted at the sky. "Back home," he repeated thoughtfully as though he were talking to a passing cloud. "Back home, she says, in Gettysburg."

"Well, and what's so funny about that?" Ann snapped.

Andy slowly brought his attention down from the sky. "You may be good at your letters," he said, "but your geography's mighty poor. Gettysburg ain't your home now, little lady. Your home is right spang here, in the Western Country, the other side of the mountains." He jutted his chin out. "Y'don't like it much, do ya?"

Ann felt the tears smarting behind her eyes. She drew herself up tall. Oh, he was hateful, hateful, she thought. Then just as she had decided to walk away without answering him, his expression changed. He dropped his eyes to the ground and all at once he looked both ashamed and sorry.

"I didn't aim to make you mad," he mumbled, shifting his feet on the ground.

Ann looked at him closely. What a strange boy! A minute ago he was acting like a rooster begging for a fight, and now he was hanging his head like a whipped dog. You thought you had him figured out one way, then he turned around and surprised you.

"With all your readin' and writin'," he was saying, "I don't suppose you care much for just— playin'?"

Ann was about to answer primly that she was generally far too busy for playing, but at the last minute she changed her mind.

"What kind of playing?" she asked.

"Well—" Andy looked almost shy. "What kind did you used to do back in Gettysburg?"

"Oh, in Gettysburg—" Ann began dreamily. As she spoke, her eyes happened to rest on the grapevine rope Andy had dropped behind him. All of a sudden she had a picture of herself and Margaret skipping rope after school.

"1, 2, 3, 4, 5, 6, 7, 8" (they would sing)
"Mary sat at the garden gate
  Eating plums from off a plate."

Ann put her book and pencil down on the road and ran for the grapevine rope. "We used to skip rope," she said. "Like this." She turned the rope quickly—over and back, over and back and skipped in a circle around Andy.

"Can you do it?" she asked breathlessly, holding the rope out to him.

Andy folded his arms deliberately across his chest. "Skip rope!" he scoffed. "Maybe in Gettysburg it's different, but where I come from—men and boys, they don't skip rope." He brought to his voice all the scorn he could gather.

Oh dear, Ann thought, now he had changed again. She should have known better. Maybe it was her turn to apologize, but before she could say anything Andy had grabbed the rope out of her hand.

"In my neck of the woods," he said gruffly, "we don't fool around with little girls' skip ropes." He turned on his heel and started down the road.

For a moment Ann felt sorry. "What do you do where you come from?" she called.

Instead of answering, Andy stopped and suddenly shot the rope out within inches of Ann's feet, then made it twirl on the ground like a snake. "Oh, by the way," he said, "my ma sent me to tell Mrs. Hamilton she's feelin' poorly. She'd take it as a favor if Mrs. Hamilton would come and sit with her."

Ann's mouth dropped open. "Andy McPhale," she called, "do you mean to tell me you've waited all this time to give me that message?"

Andy was gone, walking down the hill, swinging that old grapevine in his hand. He wasn't even headed toward his own home, Ann thought with exasperation as she turned to go back to the cabin. Oh, Andy McPhale was the worst, she decided. Of all the boys she had ever known, Andy was the worst.

Chapter Three

Ann had been asleep in the loft for what seemed a long time when she was wakened by voices in the cabin below. That must be her mother and Daniel back from the McPhales'. Ann slid closer to the loft opening.

"She never did send Andy for anyone," Daniel was explaining, to her father and David, his voice low. "She said he worries whenever she feels poorly and it's not the first time he's taken the notion to call a neighbor."

"Well, the Lord knows the poor woman needs help," Mrs. Hamilton murmured as she put down the little bag of medicine and first-aid materials she always kept ready for emergency. "That husband of hers hasn't been home for ten days. Goes out hunting and trapping like that days at a time and doesn't leave behind him enough food to hold out until he gets back."

"Nothing planted, I suppose," David observed.

"Doesn't believe in planting," Daniel grumbled. "And the kind of folks that don't plant, often don't plan either, you'll notice. No account —that's what they are."

"Yes," Mr. Hamilton agreed. "They likely couldn't make out in the East and they likely won't make out here."

Ann peeked over the edge of the loft and saw her father shaking his head. Her mother was leaning over the baby's cradle and tucking a cover around him.

"Well, I'm going down there again in the morning," she said, "and take some milk and johnny cake and a few supplies. They've hardly had a thing the last few days but berries and a couple of rabbits the boy managed to catch."

The voices below became faint. Ann moved back to her bed and closed her eyes. "No account"—the words began to turn over and over in her mind to the tune of a jump-rope rhyme. Then somewhere in the middle of the words came the hoot of an owl from down the road— or was it an owl? Whatever it was, it started out sounding long and lonely and ended up sounding lost, like all night noises. Ann shivered and pulled the quilt up over her ears.

When she woke, all the lonely night sounds had been driven away by daylight. It was going to be a good morning. Ann could hear her father announcing the weather from the open doorway as he did every sun-up.

"Fair day on Hamilton Hill. Clear sky. Not a cloud showing and work to be done." Father made his voice sound like the town crier back home who always ended his sentences like a wind dying down. Ann knew there was a chuckle behind his words and that the right side of his face would be quirked into the wonderful half-smile that meant he was pleased with the world. At this time of year, he would say, every day of sunshine was gold in your pockets. He would also say, and was, indeed, at this very moment saying, that sunshine shouldn't be wasted.

Ann jumped out of bed and in a few minutes was in the room below helping her mother ladle out the breakfast mush into wooden bowls. The three men sat in a row on the bench at the table. You could see that their minds were already at work in the fields and it was hard for them to stay behind.

Mrs. Hamilton set the first bowl of mush down in front of her husband.

"Are you still planning to go down to the Mc-Phales'?" he asked.

"Yes. Ann can pick the peas while I'm gone

and shell them and get the potatoes ready and cooking. The baby will nap most of the morning and I'll be back by noon." Mrs. Hamilton smiled at her three impatient men. "Dinner won't be late," she assured them.

After the men had gone to the fields, Mrs. Hamilton packed a basket of food. "Be sure to build up the fire," she reminded Ann as she went out the door. "Remember it's a fresh fire this morning and won't last long without care."

That was probably the most important job of all, Ann thought as she went out to the vegetable patch. She hated to think of her father's face and Daniel's face if she ever let a fire go out and had to call them in from the fields to start a new one.

She tied the bottom corners of her apron to her waist band to form a long pocket across her lap. Vegetables grew around the cabin, up to the barn, and to the edge of the clearing. Ann walked up one row of peas and down another, picking and dropping them into her folded apron pocket. It was a nice feeling to go between the straight rows, her yellow dress brushing the plants on either side, and remember that she had helped to plant these peas. Now they marched right across Hamilton Hill to where the trees began!

Her apron full, Ann sat down on the doorstep and began to shell the peas into a large wooden bowl. The empty pods she dropped on the ground beside her to be picked up later. The only sound in all the world was the snap-snapping of pea pods until all at once a redbird, bursting out of the forest, broke the loneliness with his whistle.

"Don't you whistle at me, Redbird," Ann called. "I'm much too busy to pay one bit of attention to what you say."

All the same, she whistled an answer. The redbird, delighted with company, balanced himself on a pea vine, ready to go on with the conversation, but a noise from behind startled him into flight. Out of the forest came Andy McPhale, his tousled head bent down, his arms behind him. Even so, there was a kind of swagger to Andy as he made his way between the rows of peas and came to a stop in front of Ann.

"How's your mother?" Ann asked.

"Some better," Andy replied, looking up. His

arms were still locked behind him as if he were hiding something. Whatever it was, he was grinning and seemed pleased about it.

Probably has a snake back there, Ann thought, and means to scare me. "My mother has gone down to your place," she said, pretending not to notice anything. "Did you pass her?"

Andy shook his head. "I didn't take the road. Came through the woods instead."

Then, as if he couldn't hold his secret another minute, Andy suddenly brought his hands from behind his back—and there was a wild turkey! He held it high by its feet, its head dangling.

"Just killed it with a sling shot," he said. "Big one, ain't he?" He tried to make his words matter-of-fact and everyday, but he couldn't keep the pride out.

And no wonder. A wild turkey with a sling shot! Ann smiled up at this strange boy who sometimes almost surprised her into liking him. "He's a beauty," she said. "Why don't you sit down here and clean it before you take it back to your mother? I'll get a knife."

She ran into the cabin and took a quick look

at the baby who was still napping. As she picked up the knife, her mother's words of last night flashed through her mind. "Nothing but berries and a couple of rabbits." Ann dipped out a cup of milk and broke off a large chunk of johnny cake and took them out to the doorstep.

Andy gulped down the milk and ate the johnny cake quickly. Then side by side, they went to work—Ann shelling peas, Andy plucking feathers.

Andy worked quickly and expertly but he didn't mix his work with any talk. When he had finished, he stood up, but instead of leaving, he went over to where the empty pea pods were lying and began kicking one at a time with his big toe.

Ann glanced up from the potatoes she was peeling now. "Want to help peel?" she offered.

"Naw." Andy dropped down to the ground beside the empty pods and started arranging them in different patterns.

"What are you doing?" Ann asked.

Then as she looked, she could see that Andy was making a fence with the pods. There was a

row of pods up and down, joined by a line across. The two up-and-down pieces at one end, however, had tilted toward each other, so that with the cross pod between them, they formed the letter A.

"Look, Andy," Ann pointed out. "You've made an A. That's the first letter of your name."

"Honest?" Andy's face lighted as it had when he showed Ann the turkey. "Just those three lines? That's how my name starts?"

"And here's how you make the rest of it." Ann set the bowl of potatoes down and quickly rearranged the pods to spell "Andy."

Without a word, Andy gathered up other pods and began carefully to copy the letters below the model Ann had made.

"I could teach you all the letters," Ann offered. "I could teach you how to write sometime, if you want."

In a burst of enthusiasm she went on. "Oh, Andy, why don't you folks plant? You could have a nice farm down there. I could show you how to grow peas, too."

Andy dropped the pod he was holding. He stood up and rammed his hands into his pockets. He reminded Ann of a cat who has had his fur rubbed the wrong way.

"We ain't farmin' folk," he said, his chin jutted out. "We don't always want to be tinkering in the dirt—puttin' things in the ground, pullin' them out, lookin' for sun one minute and cryin' for rain the next. We likely won't be stayin' here long anyway. We'll probably pull out when my pa gets back."

"But you don't *want* to, do you? You wouldn't want to *quit*, would you?" Ann hit the word "quit" hard like you would a nail. Her father had said the McPhales wouldn't make out, but they had hardly tried. They had been here such a short time.

"Why not?" Andy laughed. "Just what you want to do too, ain't it?"

"I would *not*," Ann replied but, even as she spoke, she felt her face growing hot. Wouldn't she? Wasn't that just what she had secretly been wanting all the time? No, she told herself, it wasn't the same at all. She didn't want to *quit*; she just wanted to go back to Gettysburg.

"I would not," Ann repeated louder than she needed to, and she picked up the pail of potatoes and took them into the cabin. "I have to see about dinner," she called over her shoulder.

As soon as she stepped inside, she had a sinking feeling in the bottom of her stomach. She had forgotten about the fire. Quickly she ran over to the hearth and sank down on her knees before a pile of black ashes and a half burned log. In desperation she blew into the fireplace, hoping to revive a hidden spark. Ashes flew out into the room and up in her face, but there wasn't a tiny glow of red anywhere.

And then the baby woke, letting out a sharp cry for attention.

"Oh, Johnny, Johnny, what will I do?" Ann moaned as she picked him up. "I can't call Father. I just *can't*."

She looked at the tinderbox beside the fireplace with its piece of steel and flint. She had never made a fire from the beginning.

She went to the door to tell Andy but he was gone. So was the turkey; so were the pea pods. When Ann called, there was no sound but the hopeful whistle of the redbird.

He hears me plain enough, Ann thought. He's just not answering. Oh, if we were only in Gettysburg, I could run over to Margaret's and borrow some fire to get ours started.

She walked back and forth in the cabin, holding the baby while she talked to herself.

"Maybe I could still borrow some. But if I went down the hill to Uncle John's, I'd have to take the baby. It wouldn't be so bad going, but coming back—carrying the baby and a pot of fire —I don't know if I could manage."

Then as Ann thought again of calling her father, she quickly made up her mind.

"I'll go to Uncle John's," she said firmly. "Maybe I can leave Johnny with Aunt Mary. Anyway, father always says you never know if you can do a thing until you try. And you can only cross one mountain at a time, he says."

Chapter Four

It was harder to carry Johnny and an empty iron pot than Ann had imagined. By the time she reached the road, her arms were aching, and when she came to her favorite sitting spot she wanted so much to stop and forget all about fires and peas and potatoes and dinner-on-time. It would be a perfect morning to sit in her half circle of trees and look down the road and dream. The road had a dancing look to it today. Little spots of sunshine trickled through the trees and grapevines, and lay flickering on the road.

Roads are different from streets, Ann thought. Streets are businesslike and only expected things happen on them, but roads have moods and mysteries and secrets to tell and promises to make around every corner. Even though the road had brought Ann nothing but hardship, still it had a way of saying, "Anything can happen here . . . you never know."

Right now Ann couldn't go on with such dreamy thoughts and ignore her arms one minute longer. She still wasn't even half way to Uncle John's. She couldn't help it; she would have to stop and rest.

Ann dropped down under a chestnut tree, put the pot down beside her, and let the baby lie in her lap. What a wonderful relief it was! She would have to stop more often, she decided, yet all the time the sun was climbing higher in the sky. When the sun reached the top of the sky and before it started to slide down the other side, it would be dinner time. The men would put down their tools and walk home.

Ann started to get up; then suddenly she laughed. How silly she had been. She didn't need to carry the iron pot at all. She could borrow one from Aunt Mary. Then if she could leave Johnny with Aunt Mary, she would have only Johnny to carry one way and only the pot to carry the other. She was looking for a place to hide the pot until she could come for it another time when over the rim of the hill came the sound of hoofbeats.

A moment later a great chestnut-colored horse climbed into sight. On the back of the horse sat a man with matching chestnut hair and he was singing. When he reached Ann, he stopped his horse and his song at the same time.

"I wondered what I would see when I came up this hill," he said. "Last thing in the world I expected was a pretty young lady with a baby in her arms."

Ann smiled, realizing that she was as much a surprise to this young man as he was to her. And then she went on smiling, because he was that kind of man. He was young, not much older than Daniel, with a shower of freckles across his nose and a face that seemed to take part in whatever he was thinking. Before she knew it, Ann had told him who she was, where she lived, where she was going, and that the fire was out.

Suddenly she remembered that her mother had said always to be careful of strangers on the road. A man traveling alone could be a hunter, a settler, or he could be a horse thief. "Oh, you're not, are you?" Ann asked in alarm. "You're not a horse thief?"

The young man threw back his head and laughed, his freckles dancing like spots of sunlight. He swung down from his saddle and made Ann a bow.

"Miss Ann," he said, talking serious now and as if Ann were a grown lady, "if your fire is out, there isn't much time for a proper introduction.

I am Arthur Scott of Lancaster County, come to the Western Country to find land and settle, and I am at your service. Now let's go build that fire."

Ann thought it would be nice to drop a curtsy to show that she knew about proper introductions and that she never really believed he was a horse thief, but a curtsy was rather difficult to manage with a baby in her arms and an iron pot hanging from one hand. Besides, Arthur Scott was already helping her up onto his horse. He had taken the baby in one arm and now he was leading the horse up the hill toward the Hamilton cabin.

Riding home on Mr. Scott's horse, Ann felt more like a queen than a barefoot girl with peas and potatoes to cook. It was partly the way Arthur Scott talked that made her feel like that. He didn't treat her as if there were lots of years between them, the way most grownups do. He talked sometimes as if she was as old as he was and sometimes as if he were just her age.

At the cabin, using his own tinderbox to start

the fire, Mr. Scott seemed just as eager as Ann to have dinner ready on time.

"It won't take long now," he said, fanning the flame high.

Ann stepped out of the door and squinted up at the sun. Yes, there would be time. She hurried over to the fire with two large pots filled with water. Arthur Scott helped her hang them over the flame and then stood up, grinning.

"I don't know why your folks need know anything about your fire going out," he said. "Why don't we keep it our secret?"

"You mean you won't tell?" Ann asked gratefully.

Mr. Scott's eyes twinkled as he leaned down close to Ann. "Never," he whispered, and suddenly they were both laughing like fellow conspirators.

"That is," Mr. Scott went on, "if you'll put my name in those pots while I walk up to your father's fields and make the proper introductions."

In the Western Country putting someone's name in the pot meant he was staying for dinner.

Other travelers had stopped from time to time at Hamilton Hill for a meal, but never anyone like Arthur Scott, Ann thought as she watched him stride across the clearing to the lower fields where her father and brothers were working. Ann wished there were something for dinner besides peas and potatoes and johnny cake. If her mother got back in time, maybe she would make some wonders. The thought of her mother's fried wonders dipped in sugar—those delicious brown cake rings with holes in the middle—made Ann's mouth water.

Maybe they could even make the dinner very special, Ann thought with mounting excitement, and use Mother's linen tablecloth and china plates with the little lavender flowers on them. Frontier folk generally didn't have anything this fancy, but because Uncle John had first settled Hamilton Hill three years ago, her father had made several trips back and forth and somehow had found room for them. They had been put aside for a party "some day," and Ann decided that this was a perfect party day. In fact, the more she thought about it, the more party-ish she felt, and all at once she knew something she could do right now. She climbed up to her private shelf and reached down her two blue satin hair ribbons. She tied a bow at the end of each of her braids and smiled to think how much difference those two little bows must make. There was no mirror on Hamilton Hill, but sometimes, Ann had discovered, if she caught the light just right, she could find her reflection in a pail of water. She moved a pail over to the light by the doorway and was looking in the water, first on one side, then on the other, when her mother came up behind her.

"Oh, Mother," Ann exclaimed, pushing the pail aside, "can we have a party dinner? Will you make a batch of wonders? And can we, please, use the tablecloth and china plates?" Once Ann started to tell her mother about Arthur Scott and her plans for dinner, her words tumbled out faster and faster, picking up more words as they went—the way a few pebbles sometimes start a landslide down a mountain.

"Wait a minute!" Her mother laughed, holding up her hands. "You know what your father says when your ideas run away with you."

Ann nodded. If her father were here now, he would say, "Whoa, there, girl—one mountain at a time!" Then he would help her look at her plans slowly and when he had finished, the plans might all be changed and the excitement gone.

"But, Mother . . ." Ann began and then she noticed how hot and tired her mother looked. Mrs. Hamilton brushed a lock of hair off her forehead as she leaned over the fireplace to look into the pots.

"No, Ann," she said patiently. "We can't have a party in the middle of the day with work to be done. Arthur Scott is welcome to share whatever we have, the way we always have it, and I expect even he would think we were mighty foolish to set a fancy table on a Monday noon."

Ann hadn't thought of it that way, and although she secretly suspected her mother might be right, still it was disappointing and tiresome. Peas and potatoes on the same old wooden plates *again!* Ann slapped six plates around the table and wondered how anything important enough for lavender flowered china could ever happen on the western side of the mountains.

When Arthur Scott tramped into the cabin with the three Hamilton men, however, Ann forgot her disappointment. The men were all laughing together, and Ann could tell right away that her father thought Arthur Scott was nicer than most travelers. Meeting Mr. Scott seemed to make Mrs. Hamilton feel better, too.

"This is our daughter, Ann," Mr. Hamilton said.

Mr. Scott bowed, giving Ann a private wink. "I have had the pleasure," he said. "I stopped in at the cabin and Miss Ann agreed to put my name in the pot."

But when they sat down at the table Ann felt like a little girl again. Everyone began talking politics and Ann couldn't find her way into the conversation at all. Of course children were not supposed to be heard at the table but politics made even listening dull. Ann let her mind wander off by itself until something Mr. Scott said suddenly made her take notice. He was talking about the war that was just over. "When I was at Valley Forge—" he said. Without thinking, Ann jumped right into the middle of his sentence.

"Were you a soldier at Valley Forge?" Even if Daniel did scowl at her for interrupting, Ann didn't care. As far back as she could remember, she had heard stories about the terrible winter at Valley Forge, but never before from anyone who had been there.

"I was only thirteen years old," Mr. Scott said. "They wouldn't take me as a soldier so I drove an ammunition wagon."

Ann stole a look at Daniel. He was still scowling. He stepped warningly on her foot under the table. Ann moved her foot aside and turned again to Mr. Scott.

"How were you ever brave enough to stay all winter?" she asked, hoping no one would stop her.

"Ann, you forget yourself," Daniel began, but Mrs. Hamilton put her hand quietly on Daniel's arm and leaned forward to hear what Arthur Scott had to say.

Mr. Scott spoke slowly, as if he were sending his mind back six years to remember just how it was. "I guess I would have been ashamed to quit when there was so much bravery all around me. I remember a girl," he said, speaking directly to Ann, "who wasn't as big as you are. Her name was Rachel Peck and she lived nearby. All winter she used to save food from her own plate and make gingerbread every chance she had. She would walk through snow up to her knees to bring that food to the soldiers."

Ann swallowed hard. She would have done that, too, she thought. If she'd been there, she would have gone in snow up to her waist. She moved to the edge of the bench. "And did you ever see General Washington?"

Arthur Scott's face lighted up. "Yes," he said. "Whenever our courage began to peter out, General Washington always seemed to know. We would suddenly find him there in the midst of us. And all we had to do was to look in his face to remember why we were there. I never could figure out how just looking at a man could make a person feel bigger and better and stronger, but that's the way it was. A soldier would go through a heap of suffering to keep from disappointing General Washington."

Ann found herself feeling all trembly inside. It was almost as if General Washington had stepped into the cabin—impossible as that was. General Washington belonged on the other side of the mountains where all the excitement was. Where important things happened—things that would get written down in history.

Ann pictured General Washington as he must have been at Valley Forge, riding a white horse or perhaps walking through the snow. Nothing about him was very clear except his face. Even though she had never seen a picture, she felt sure that now she knew just what General Washington's face looked like. She was so deep in her thoughts that she didn't notice that dinner was over, and that while the men were standing in the doorway, talking, she was sitting at the table alone. Then she thought of one more question.

"Mr. Scott," she said and jumped up from the table and ran to the doorway, "you are going to stay for a while, aren't you?"

Ann didn't know what the men had been talking about before she interrupted. All she knew was that all at once it was very quiet. Daniel was standing on the step in front of the others. The silence seemed to be more because of Daniel's sudden thunderous look than because of anything Ann had done. Daniel turned on her.

"If no one else will correct you, I will," he said, his eyes flashing. "You have done nothing but interrupt your elders and act as if you had never been taught otherwise. You've lost your Eastern manners, Ann Hamilton, and talk as bold as any common Western girl." Daniel turned his back on the group. He had said his say and even the way he held his shoulders showed that he knew he was right.

Ann cringed. She didn't dare look at Mr. Scott. The silence seemed to grow so thick, she felt choked by it and wanted to run away. Far away.

But then she felt a hand on her arm and there was David. He had stepped back beside her and was grinning and winking and secretly pointing to the pail of water Ann had left near the door. He put his finger over his lips. David was going to try and catch Daniel in some fault-finding. Mr. Hamilton stepped back and whispered something in Arthur Scott's ear. All at once the silence at the door stopped being unfriendly, and Ann put her hand quietly in David's.

"I haven't noticed anything wrong with Western ladies," David remarked innocently, reaching down with one hand toward the pail.

"They are not ladies," Daniel snapped, his back still turned. "The only ladies here are those fresh from the East. Most girls who have been here a spell shed their manners with their shoes. And I don't want any sister of mine taking on unbecoming Western ways."

Daniel started to stride away when all of a sudden there was a great hoot from David. A pailful of cold spring water hit Daniel square on the back, dripped down his collar, rolled down the length of his sleeves, and settled in a pool around his feet.

Daniel swung around to face David. He must have said some angry words but no one could hear them. Everyone was laughing. David was shouting that this was what happened if you found fault with Western girls and Western manners. The laughter didn't seem to be so much at Daniel as it was the laughter that comes at the end of a long standing joke. Daniel, as he calmed down and shook off water, had to admit he had been caught fair and square. Mr. and Mrs. Hamilton and Arthur Scott smiled as they watched the two brothers spar, half in play, half in earnest. Ann sat down on the step, filled with gratitude and relief. Everyone had forgotten about her. She grinned as she remembered the loud smack the water had made as it hit Daniel in the back.

Chapter Five

THERE is nothing like a family dunking to make everyone feel at home. It turned out that Arthur Scott was looking for land right in the same county, and the Hamiltons invited him to make their cabin his headquarters as long as he was around. Sometimes he would be gone for two or three days to the western part of the county. At those times Ann noticed that she wasn't the only one who stopped on the doorstep to glance toward the road and she wasn't the only one who listened for hoofbeats. Everyone felt better when Arthur Scott was there.

One morning before Mr. Scott left on his business, he went to the edge of the clearing to chop firewood for Mrs. Hamilton. Ann went along. She took her knitting and sat down on a stump near Mr. Scott. Ann had a lot of questions to ask, but there was one that was especially important. She finished a row of stitches, put down her needles, and waited for Arthur Scott to straighten up between blows of his axe.

"Mr. Scott," she said, "why did you ever want to come on this side of the mountains to settle?"

Arthur Scott sank his axe into a log and left it there. When he lifted his head, Ann recognized that same look of excitement that Daniel had had and David and her father and Uncle John when they had first talked of the West.

"Land," Arthur Scott replied briefly. "More land than I could ever afford in the East and a stake in a new part of the country."

Ann picked up her knitting again. Land. It was the same disappointing answer that the Hamilton men gave. Why would anyone give up a working farm and good neighbors and a school and a church for a lot of uncleared land?

"Some day you will understand," Arthur Scott said. "Some day this hill will mean so much to you, you wouldn't leave it even if you had the chance."

Ann was about to say what she thought of Mr. Scott's "some day" when there was a sudden muffled snort behind her. Turning around, she saw Andy McPhale hiding behind a tree. He had been listening to every word and he was laughing at what Arthur Scott had said.

"Come on out, Andy, I see you," Ann called sharply, but already Andy was bounding away and heading for cover.

"Why, that's the same boy that's been spying on me ever since I've been here," Arthur Scott exclaimed in surprise. "Every time I ride down the hill, I see him peeping out from behind a bush or staring down from a tree."

"He's strange," Ann explained. She realized now that Andy hadn't come around at all since Arthur Scott had been there. At least he hadn't come in sight. Later, when Ann walked back to the cabin with Mr. Scott, she looked over her shoulder and saw Andy again. He was following them in the distance, darting from tree to tree.

After that whenever Arthur Scott was around, Ann was aware of mysterious sounds—a branch creaking, a padded footstep, a stone rolling. Then one day Arthur Scott said he wouldn't be back for several weeks. He had found land on the other side of Catfish Camp, so far west that Indians still came there. He needed to take care of the deed, and he wanted to do a little clearing before he went back East. After the winter, he planned to bring his father back and settle.

That evening when Mr. Scott had left for his new land, Andy McPhale came out of hiding.

He walked right up to the Hamilton's open door while they were eating supper and knocked.

"Come in, Andy," Mr. Hamilton invited.

"I brought you something." Andy stepped in and held out an enormous piece of venison. "My pa's back. He killed two deer. He says to give this to you and thank you kindly for helping us out while he was gone." Andy rushed from one sentence to another as if he wanted to get it over. "We're movin' on soon," he said, taking a big breath. "Goin' back where we came from. After a few weeks—when Ma gets a little stronger." Andy started to leave.

Mr. Hamilton glanced over at his wife, who nodded as if she were agreeing to something they had talked about before.

"Come back a minute, Andy," Mr. Hamilton called. "I have a proposition for you and your father. Ask him if he would like to give us a hand with our work on the hill as long as he's around. We're going to finish clearing and plough the south field for a fall planting of rye. In return you folks can help yourself to all the vegetables you can eat and fresh milk every day. You're big enough to help out too, Andy. We'll figure out some special payment for you, if you've a mind to."

Andy's eyes were alight. "I've a mind to," he answered quickly. "And I know a payment." Suddenly his face flushed a bright red as if he had heard himself say something he hadn't known he was going to say. He turned and ran out of the cabin. As he went, Ann saw sticking out of his back pocket a bunch of old pea pods.

She followed Andy out of the door and stopped him in front of the cabin.

"What kind of payment were you thinking of?" she asked.

"Nothin'," he grunted, turning away from her.

The pea pods looked crumpled, Ann noticed, as if they had been handled a lot. "You know," she said, "I'd give you writing lessons any time you wanted. You wouldn't need to pay for that."

Andy studied his bare toes and when he spoke Ann could hardly hear him. "What I was thinkin'," he said, "is I'd like to work for your pa in return for writin' lessons."

"Well, let's begin right now," Ann said cheerfully, "only I have one question to ask you first, Andy McPhale. Why did you hide and spy on Arthur Scott while he was here?"

Andy didn't look up. "Didn't like him," he said. "I wanted him to go. I couldn't ask for lessons as long as he was here. Besides, you wouldn't want to talk to me when there was an eddicated man around." Andy looked at Ann with some of his old defiance. "Now, would you, Miss Gettysburg?" he said.

Ann sighed in exasperation and picked up a stick. Marking in the bare dirt next to the cabin, she wrote down the letters of the alphabet. "Here's your first lesson," she said.

After that, every day when Andy and Mr. McPhale came up the hill to work for Mr. Hamilton, Andy would stop off for a lesson. In the evening he would stop again. Before long he was putting letters together to make words and then he took to experimenting on his own with words. As he went past the cabin, he would scratch a word in the dirt, leaving it there for Ann to find and correct the spelling. One day Ann found beside the door a whole sentence:

GETISBERG is ELiGENT

Ann smiled and picked up a stick to make corrections. She wrote:

GETTYSBURG is VERY ELEGANT

All the time that Andy was learning, he seemed to be changing in other ways, too. Ann noticed that he seemed to walk straighter. He didn't hang his head so much and he wasn't forever looking for a fight.

The summer days drifted away. The blackberries ripened beside the road and the corn in Mr. Hamilton's field reached up to Daniel's shoulders.

Then one day Arthur Scott came back. It was evening. Ann and Andy were sitting on the steps and Ann was reciting the rule about "i before e except after c" when there was the sound of hoofbeats and Arthur Scott was riding up to the cabin. Ann dropped the stick she was using and ran to meet him.

As Mr. Scott swung down from his saddle, he found himself surrounded by Hamiltons who had heard him and come from all directions. David came out of the barn and held out his hand.

"Welcome, neighbor," he grinned. "You must be a full-fledged land owner now, and that makes you a neighbor even if you are on the other side of the county. Guess we'll have to get up early in the morning when we take Sunday dinner with you."

Everyone was laughing and talking and it was a few minutes before Ann noticed that Andy McPhale had disappeared. She shrugged her shoulders. If he was going to be so silly, she wasn't going to waste time thinking about it.

There was such a little time to be with Arthur Scott anyway. He was leaving the next morning. All the Hamiltons seemed to be aware of the short time left with their good friend and of the long, lonely winter ahead. That evening there was more gaiety on the hill than there had ever been. The laughter and jokes and stories stretched out long after candlelighting, long after they would normally be in bed.

The next morning Arthur Scott was gone. Just before he left, he leaned down from his horse and whispered to Ann. "Don't let that fire go out," he said, "before I come back next spring." Then he urged his horse forward and in a moment all that could be seen of Arthur Scott was a shadow of dust on the long, long road East.

That day was an empty day and a long one at Hamilton Hill. The sun seemed unusually warm, the chores especially tiresome. Ann had the sensation that the hill was an island floating farther and farther away from the rest of the world. Even the road had no magic to it that day.

Ann didn't bother to go to the road in the evening when she took down her diary. She sat on the doorstep, thinking that Andy might come along for a lesson. While she waited, she thought about Arthur Scott and tried to remember everything that had happened since she had met him on the road. She thought of that first dinner and his stories about Valley Forge. She picked up her pencil and wrote in her diary.

"We must seem very ordinary to Arthur Scott, who has seen General Washington and been with such brave folks. But if I had the same chance as Rachel Peck, I would be brave too. I would not mind snow either, if I were doing something important. Instead, look where I am and what I am doing. On a forsaken hill in the Western Country, tending a vegetable patch."

Suddenly Ann felt as if someone were in the doorway close behind her, looking over her shoulder. She snapped her diary shut. David was standing at her back, gazing innocently over her head at the summer sky.

"I declare it looks like snow," he drawled. "I believe you better bake a batch of gingerbread, Sister Ann."

Ann whirled around. "You've been reading what I wrote," she choked. "You—you *snoop!*"

Ann dropped her diary on the step and started to run toward the road. It was then that she noticed the letters scratched by the cabin.

Good Ridence

Andy had, of course, been thinking of Arthur Scott. Ann scuffed up the letters angrily before she went on. She didn't see two eyes peering out from a bush near the cabin. All she wanted was to be alone where she could feel sad or she could feel mad without interference.

Chapter Six

THE next morning Mrs. Hamilton took the baby and a basket of quilting squares and went down the hill to see her sister-in-law, Mary Hamilton. Ann could have gone, too, if she had wanted to—as long as she was back in time to carry lunch to the men in the south field. The ploughing was almost done now, but because this field was so far from the cabin, Ann had been taking the noon meal down every day.

72

She didn't want to go to Aunt Mary's. Ladies' talk was often just as dull as politics, and besides, Ann didn't like to quilt. Instead, she spent the morning on her hands and knees weeding around the vegetables. It felt good to turn up the rich, brown earth and to work until her back and arms ached. Sometimes when she worked like this, Ann felt it was the strength from her own body that was making the vines so stout and healthy and turning the pumpkins golden. She felt her own hard work going down into the ground and making the potatoes grow. She worked until time to go to the fields with lunch.

David saw Ann first as she approached with a pail of food in each hand. He dropped his hoe and started to meet her.

"Come on, boys," he called loudly. "Here's little Rachel Peck with a pail of gingerbread."

Ann stopped right where she was. She put the two pails down at her feet and turned around to go home. David could hand out the food and bring the empty pails home when he came. She wouldn't stay and visit if he was going to poke

73

fun at her. Ann walked slowly up the hill, past the flax field, the cornfield, the barn, through the vegetable garden, to the cabin.

She sat down on the step with a cup of milk and a piece of cold meat and felt very, very sorry for herself. Arthur Scott was gone, Andy was being hateful again, and David was teasing. Ann went to get her diary. At least now she could write what she pleased without anyone looking over her shoulder.

When she reached up to the shelf, the diary wasn't there. She felt along the whole length of the shelf—first quickly, frantically, then slowly and carefully. She took down Semanthie and the Gettysburg shoes and the blue ribbons, and then the shelf was bare.

Ann thought back to the night before. She remembered, then, that she had left the diary on the step when she had gone down to the road. She searched in front of the cabin. She looked through the inside of the cabin. It wasn't there. David must have picked it up and hidden it as part of his joke on her. Well, she wouldn't ask him. It would only mean more teasing. She would have to get along without it until he felt like giving it back.

Suddenly Ann wanted Margaret more than she ever had in all the time she had been here. Two tears started in her eyes and rolled slowly down her cheeks. Oh, she was lonesome for girl-talk and girl-play and a girl!

She looked at Semanthie staring up from the table where she had been dropped. Ann thought of the times that Semanthie had been along when she and Margaret had dressed up and played house. They would sneak off from the boys and give make-believe tea parties with their dolls. All afternoon it would be "Good day, Mrs. Jones," and "How are your children, Mrs. Smith? Keeping well, I hope." Oh, it had been lovely . . . lovely.

All at once Ann dried her eyes. She was going to have a tea party right now. She would find a pretty place in the woods where she could set out a pretend table and gather pretend food. It wouldn't be the same alone with just Semanthie, but she was going to do it anyway. And she was going to dress up.

Ann tied the blue ribbons on her hair. She put on a fresh pink apron, her long white stockings, and she sat down to put on her blue Gettysburg shoes. She started with her right foot. She put her toes into the shoe and pulled. And she pulled. She unlaced as far as she could unlace and pulled again. Her foot simply would not go in. She couldn't squeeze it in. In one summer her feet had grown too big. And all the time her Gettysburg shoes had been sitting on the shelf —wasted.

Ann felt the tears starting again but she brushed them away impatiently. No matter what, she was going to have a fancy tea party. If she couldn't wear her shoes, she would take something else to make the party special. As she slipped off her white stockings to go barefoot, her eyes lighted on her mother's chest in one corner of the cabin. This was the chest that was never opened, that was waiting for "some day." It had her father's silver buckled shoes in it, her mother's silk dress, the linen tablecloth and the twelve lavender flowered plates. Quickly Ann made up her mind. If no one else would use the plates, she would.

Carefully she opened the chest and un-wrapped two of the lavender flowered plates—one for herself and one for Semanthie. The plates were even more beautiful than Ann had remembered—and so thin! She would take good care of them. When she finished with them, she would wrap them up just the way she had found them. No one need ever know that two lavender flowered plates had been used this afternoon at a tea party on Hamilton Hill.

Carrying the plates in one hand and Seman-thie in the other, Ann went out the door of the cabin. Behind her the Gettysburg shoes and white stockings lay on the floor where she had left them. The lid of her mother's chest gaped open. It didn't matter, Ann thought. She would be back in plenty of time to straighten up before anyone else came home.

Beyond the pea vines and the pumpkins, at

the edge of the woods that led down to the McPhales', there was a perfect place for a tea party. Enough trees had been cut down so that there was room to spread a party; enough trees stayed up to keep a party secret. Standing, Ann could see the cabin, but once she sat down, she and Semanthie and the flowered plates and the tea party would be hidden in a world all their own.

She propped Semanthie up against a stump. In front of Semanthie stretched a soft green velvet tablecloth of moss. In the center of the moss tablecloth Ann arranged three pine cones and a spray of fern as decoration. Then at Semanthie's place and her own, Ann set the lavender flowered plates.

Already the party looked beautiful. Ann ran back and forth, bringing wild grapes to put on the flowered plates, placing large leaves on the table as extra serving pieces. On one of the leaves she arranged a handful of acorns. She filled another with red dogwood berries which looked just like the little cinnamon candies she used to have back home in Gettysburg.

Ann stood looking critically down at the table. If only Margaret were here! For a moment she hesitated to sit down. It was so very quiet. When she started party-talk with Semanthie, was it going to seem lonely—just her own voice in the big woods?

She looked around for something more to add to the table. As she did so, she happened to glance toward the cabin. Coming out of the door and heading straight for the tea party was Mrs. Hamilton.

Ann didn't move. There was no use; her mother had seen her. She could try to hide the flowered plates but that wouldn't be any use either. Her mother had already been in the cabin and seen the open chest.

Ann waited, her heart pounding and her eyes on the ground. When she finally looked up, her mother was standing quietly beside her and looking at the tea party table. Ann held her breath, but for some reason her mother didn't look cross at all. Instead, there was the same kind of lovingness in her face as she had when she rocked the baby after he had been crying for a long time. Then Mrs. Hamilton turned to Ann and smiled.

"Good afternoon, Mrs. Jones," she said. "I hope I am not too late for tea. And is this your daughter?" Mrs. Hamilton nodded toward Semanthie. "My, how she's grown!"

All at once Ann's throat felt tight with love and gratitude. Quickly she moved Semanthie's flowered plate in front of her mother and gave Semanthie an oak leaf.

"Oh, do sit down, Mrs. Smith," Ann said. "And will you have cream or lemon in your tea?"

She poured cups of make-believe tea from a make-believe silver teapot. A brown rabbit stopped near the table and looked with interest before moving on. Somewhere a squirrel chattered noisily. A redbird made himself at home on a branch of a yellow elm nearby. And the two ladies daintily sipped the afternoon away and talked the loveliest party talk—all about hus-

bands and disobedient children and new babies and stylish hats.

"And have you heard," Ann's mother asked in her most fashionable voice, "that my brother-in-law, Mr. John Hamilton, is going East soon for salt and supplies? I do believe I shall ask him to bring back a pair of new shoes for my daughter. Her feet grow so."

Ann covered up a smile behind the oak leaf she was using for a fan. "Blue shoes would be lovely," she said. "I am sure your daughter would like blue shoes."

The sun had dropped low and the trees were throwing long shadows across the velvet moss and vegetable garden when Mrs. Hamilton and Ann gathered up Semanthie and the flowered plates to go back to the cabin. Ann took a last look back into the woods before she left. As she looked, the redbird dropped down onto the green moss and began to eat from the leaf filled with dogwood berries. Ann caught her breath at the beauty of it. Strange—she had never really noticed before how lovely the woods were on Hamilton Hill.

When Ann and her mother reached the cabin, they found Mr. Hamilton, David, and Daniel already there. Daniel was glowering.

"Are you aware of how late it is?" he asked.

Mrs. Hamilton handed Ann the plates to put away. Then she turned and faced her three impatient men on the doorstep. "Once in a while," she said decisively, "there comes a time in the Western Country when there is something more important than an hour of work or a meal on time."

Mrs. Hamilton went inside to prepare supper.

Chapter Seven

T<small>HE</small> happy glow from the tea party stayed with Ann for days. Everything seemed to go better. David stopped teasing and even went out of his way to be nice. One evening as he saddled the two horses to give them their exercise, he invited Ann to come along for a ride. It was one of those clear, beautiful September days when the sun can hardly bear to leave the world and when it does, it sends up a harvest moon just as round and golden as it is.

David and Ann rode down the eastern side of the hill, past Uncle John Hamilton's cabin.

"Don't come this far alone for a while, Ann," David said. "The Doane gang is loose in the county—probably farther west but better not take any chances."

"I'll be careful," Ann promised. "But tell me, David, if a man's a horse thief, can you tell just by looking at him?"

David smiled. "Generally if a man's wicked, he can't keep the wickedness out of his face any more than a good man can hide his goodness. But don't count on that. Second-rate material can be tied up in a pretty package, too. Just don't get friendly with any strangers for a while."

As David talked, he turned his horse off the road into the woods. "We're taking a short cut," he said. "I want to show you something."

Ann had never been through these woods before. The trees were bigger than they were on the top of the hill. The two horses wove their way in and out among them while Ann and David reached for clusters of wild grapes whenever they dangled low.

"Taste good," David mumbled as he popped a grape into his mouth. "Wild grapes are a sure sign of rich soil."

Pretty soon, Ann thought, he's going to tell me where he has hidden my diary. Maybe he had the diary with him. Maybe for some strange reason he has even hidden it over here and that was where they were going.

David pulled up his horse on the banks of a wild creek that suddenly broke the woods in two.

"Here we are," he said. The ground was so rocky now that only a few scattered trees were able to find a foothold. Great slabs of rock hung out over the creek and formed caves. David was looking toward the valley.

"See the place way down there where the creek meets the road? Look at that flat stretch of valley to the left of the creek. Pretty, isn't it?"

David smiled. "That's the spot where we're going to build our church some day."

Ann looked at David's face, so proud and dreaming and happy, and she looked at the piece of land he was pointing to. She tried to picture a little log church nestling there, but the trees kept getting in the way.

"It will be nice," Ann said.

"Father, Daniel, Uncle John, and I decided the other day that was the spot it should be when the time comes."

"Is that all you wanted to show me?" Ann asked.

"That's it," David nodded, his eyes still on the valley.

"It's nice," Ann repeated. Maybe on the way home David would tell her about the diary. Surely he would.

But all the way home David didn't mention it. A golden pumpkin of a moon came up and turned the road into a strange and shimmering river. Perhaps the moonlight put everything else out of David's mind.

Tomorrow, Ann thought, as she went to bed—tomorrow if he doesn't say anything, I'll ask him.

The next morning it was clear right from the beginning that it was going to be an unusual day. When Mr. Hamilton went to the door to look at the weather, he went all the way outside and stayed a while. When he came in, he didn't call out his report in his town crier voice. He just mumbled to himself and shook his head. "Queer day," he said. "Mighty queer."

After breakfast, when Ann went outside to see for herself, she had to admit that the day was, indeed, queer. Long strings of gray clouds raced across the sky. The wind sighed and moaned along the tops of trees, but down below where Ann stood there was no wind at all. The air was still . . . motionless . . . waiting. A crow dropped down to the ground as if he had been thrown there and stood, breathless and confused in the quiet.

Ann drew the shawl she was wearing closer around her shoulders. Then she saw Andy, walking toward the barn, leaning forward into a wind that strangely wasn't there. Suddenly Ann didn't want to be alone for one more minute.

"Andy!" she called. "Wait a minute!" She ran to meet him and caught up to him by the barn.

"What do you want?" he asked.

Ann hesitated. She certainly didn't want him to know that for a moment she had been frightened by a peculiar wind and a black crow.

"You haven't come for lessons," she said.

Andy leaned against the barn. "Thought you were mad. You kicked up the last letters I wrote. I was hidin' and I saw you. You were plenty mad then."

"Yes, and for good reason," Ann snapped.

Andy looked at the sky. "Still mad?" he asked.

"Oh, I guess not so much." Ann thought she had never seen clouds stream across the sky so fast.

Andy broke off a piece of long grass and put it in his mouth. "I won't have time for more lessons anyhow," he said. "We're leavin' in a day or so. We're goin' over the mountains with your Uncle John when he goes East for supplies."

Andy spit out the grass he was chewing. "I've got a piece of news," he said. He picked up a pebble from the ground and threw it as far as he could into the woods. Then he picked up another and tried to throw it even farther.

He's acting with his piece of news like he did with the wild turkey, Ann thought—hiding it behind his back as long as he can.

"Well, what is it?" Ann asked.

"We're comin' back in the spring," Andy announced proudly, "and we're a-goin' to plant. After workin' with your father, Pa thinks a farm isn't such a bad idea."

"Oh, Andy, I'm so glad," Ann cried. "And I'll help you with your vegetable garden. You'll see."

Andy picked up another pebble. This time he threw it high and it went singing off into the treetops.

"That ain't all," he said. "Pa says I kin go to

school this winter. When I come back, I'll likely be as eddicated as your old Arthur Scott."

Andy filled his hands with small stones and rattled them together like marbles. "Say," he said suddenly, "why don't you come East too for the winter? You could go with us, stay with your Cousin Margaret, and come back when we do?"

Ann drew in her breath sharply. "Oh, I couldn't," she said.

"Why not?" Andy tossed the stones up and down in his hand. "It would only be for the winter. Not much to do on a farm in the winter anyway."

Only for the winter, Ann repeated to herself. Like a visit. Then she shook her head. "They'd never let me."

"You don't know until you ask, do you?" Andy began firing his stones one after another into the woods. "Why don't you ask?"

"Maybe I will," Ann whispered slowly. All at once she was feeling as peculiar as the weather. Thoughts were streaking across her mind like the clouds in the sky. Did she really want to ask? Oh, but suppose they would allow her to go! Suppose—

"You want to go, don't you?" Andy interrupted.

Of course. It was what she had always wanted, Ann thought. Only now why did she feel so mixed up?

"Just ask your folks," Andy repeated. "I've gotta hurry. It's goin' to storm fierce before the day's over."

Some of the clouds had long, black ragged tails now, Ann noticed as she walked back to the cabin. The woods were swaying back and forth in one great movement. And the trees looked larger and taller than ever before. In comparison, the straight little rows of pea vines seemed puny and frail. The cabin seemed lost.

Mrs. Hamilton rushed out of the cabin door, carrying some sacks.

"We'll have to go to the cornfield and help pick all the corn we can before the storm hits," she said. "Then you are to pick peas and save as much as possible of the vegetable garden. This is not going to be an ordinary storm, Ann."

"What about the baby?" Ann asked, as she turned and followed her mother.

"He's asleep. He'll just have to stay alone this time until we get back." Mrs. Hamilton was almost running now.

The first gust of wind swept down from the sky. It didn't last long; it was more like a warning. Mrs. Hamilton picked up her long skirts and ran.

As Ann hurried along behind, it came to her with a shock how small, how very small her mother was. Suddenly she felt like a deserter, letting her thoughts secretly run off to Gettysburg. But it wouldn't be deserting, she reminded herself sternly. It was only for a visit.

Only for a visit, Ann repeated as she and her mother joined the Hamilton men, Andy, and Mr. McPhale in the cornfield. Only for a visit, Ann said to herself every time she dropped an ear of corn into her sack. Just a few months with Margaret. Sharing a bedroom and secrets together. Walking arm in arm to church. Trading calico squares for doll dresses. Correcting each other's copybooks.

It was such a beautiful dream that Ann forgot about the weather until all at once the sky itself seemed to drop down on Hamilton Hill. The rain came in one great sheet and lashed the hill first from one side, then another. In the cornfield people and cornstalks both bent low.

Mr. Hamilton tried to shout orders, and when he couldn't be heard, he ran from one to another. He sent Andy and his father down the hill to bring Mrs. McPhale and what possessions they could carry to the cabin. Their shack was too flimsy to hold up against the wind if it should start in earnest. He sent Mrs. Hamilton and Ann home. He and the boys stayed to finish the corn and take it to the barn.

Ann and her mother fought their way step by step against the rain. When they reached the door of the cabin, Ann turned to look at her vegetable garden.

There were her poor peas tossing back and

forth, crumpling with each new sweep of the rain! Tears rushed to Ann's eyes. The straight little rows were being dashed to the ground.

"I'll be back in a few minutes," Ann said to her mother and started off for the garden.

"It's too late," her mother called. "We'll rescue what we can later."

Ann kept on. She turned once and put her hands to her mouth and shouted, "I'll pick what I can. When the wind gets bad, I'll come in."

Ann dropped on her hands and knees in the mud beside the tattered pea vines. She picked what she could find and filled her soaking apron. All the time the rain beat down on her back and tears streamed down her face. "Oh, I hate this Western Country," she sobbed. "I hate it, I hate it."

Each time her apron was filled, Ann went to the cabin and emptied the peas inside. Each time, in spite of her mother's urgings, she went back to the vegetable garden. She worked until after the McPhales had come to the cabin. The neat little garden lay battered and broken, but still Ann worked on.

Then the wind started. It blew the rain right off the hill and set to work on the trees. Branches snapped and crackled, and Ann picked up her last apron load and went to the cabin.

As she opened the door, her mother and Mr. McPhale stood ready to bar it quickly behind her. Andy and Mrs. McPhale were on the other side of the cabin, trying to soak up with rags the water that was seeping in on the floor.

Ann stood still for a moment to catch her breath while water poured off her into a pool at her feet. Then she dropped the last apronful of peas on top of the others she had brought in. She looked at the big mound of wet peas, shreds of vines still clinging here and there.

I never want to plant another row of peas, she thought desperately. Never in all my life.

Mrs. Hamilton lifted the wet shawl gently from Ann's shoulders. She took a dry cloth and wiped Ann's face.

"I don't know what I would do without you,

Ann," she said. "I don't know what I'd do without one girl on Hamilton Hill." She unbraided
Ann's hair and rubbed it with a cloth. "I'm
proud of you. You're a brave girl."

Ann bit her lip to keep it from trembling.
Brave, her mother said. If her mother only knew
what she had been thinking! She squeezed her
mother's hand, turned quickly, and climbed the
ladder to the loft. She changed to dry clothes,
combed her hair, and slowly came down into
the cabin.

The water was blowing in under the door.
Andy was on his knees, mopping it up, when
Ann came down the ladder. She picked up a
cloth her mother had laid out and went to
help him.

"I'm not going, Andy," she said as she kneeled
down on the floor. "I'm not even going to ask."

The next few hours were a blur. Ann went
through the motions of mopping up water, of
building up the fire, of helping to peel potatoes
for dinner—and yet how silly it all seemed when

any minute the roof might be blown off or the cabin itself swept off the hill.

Mr. Hamilton, Daniel, and David stayed in the barn. Between blasts of wind Ann could hear the horses whinnying in fright. Everywhere there was noise. The screaming of wind. The creaking, groaning, cracking of trees. And sometimes a final, terrible crash.

Finally the wind stopped—not quite all at once but the way a child stops crying, wearing himself out with sobs farther and farther apart. As soon as it had quieted, the three Hamilton men burst into the cabin.

For a moment there was a confusion of talk, laughter, and tears. Mrs. Hamilton put her hand on her husband's shoulder.

"Tell us," she said, "what is left on the hill?"

Mr. Hamilton moved in front of the fire and motioned for everyone to gather around. The McPhales and the Hamilton boys took benches. Mrs. Hamilton sat in the chair beside the crib and held the baby. Ann dropped to the floor at her father's feet and held out her hands to the warmth of the fire. Mr. Hamilton's face took a serious, go-to-meeting look.

"We have much to be thankful for," he said. "We were able to save a good part of our corn. The late crop we have, of course, lost. There will be work to do over again in the south field. I see Ann has saved many of the peas, although they would have kept on bearing for a while yet. Some potatoes and pumpkin may yet be rescued. The barn and the cabin held up well. What is most important—we are here. Hamilton Hill still stands. We must thank God for His mercy."

Ann looked at her father, the firelight playing on his uplifted face, his clothes muddy and torn from the storm. His eyes seemed to be looking through the cabin and beyond it, as he tipped back his head and began reciting from the Bible.

"The Lord is my shepherd," he said. "I shall not want. He maketh me to lie down in green pastures. He leadeth me beside the still waters."

This was her father's favorite psalm, the one

he had repeated in family prayers, time and again since they had started West. It was his way of saying that he believed God had led them to the Western Country and was watching over Hamilton Hill.

Ann liked the psalm too, although there were parts that she didn't understand. Like "My cup runneth over." Her father said that meant you felt more happiness than you could possibly hold. He said there was no better way you could say this. To Ann, it seemed a strange way to talk about happiness.

"Surely goodness and mercy shall follow me all the days of my life," Mr. Hamilton went on.

It came to Ann with a kind of awe that her father was not the least discouraged by the storm. He was truly only thankful. His whole heart belonged on Hamilton Hill. Ann wished that she could be like that. There always seemed to be so many different feelings going on in her at the same time and they were all mixed up. When she tried to feel thankful, all she could think of was her flattened rows of peas that would have kept on bearing until frost.

Chapter Eight

ONE side of the McPhale shack had been blown in by the storm and an oak tree lay across their doorway. So the McPhales stayed with the Hamiltons, and Andy and his father helped clean up the hill.

Then one morning at dawn Uncle John Hamilton and the McPhales left to cross the mountains. The whole eastern half of the sky was aglow with a pink-and-gold sunrise as Ann stood on the road, waving. Somehow she felt she was saying good-bye to more than Uncle John and the McPhales. She was saying good-bye all over again to Margaret, to a visit and a dream. She was saying good-bye to the summer, too. Travel on the road was all one way now, from west to east. New settlers striking West for the first time would not be using the road again until spring. Although it was only the middle of September, Ann could already feel the loneliness of the winter creeping up the sides of the hill. She kept waving for a moment even after the road was empty.

It was not until she got back to the cabin that she discovered the letters scratched in the dirt by the door. Andy must have written them when she wasn't looking.

LUK UNDER THE STEP

There was a small opening at the back of the

cabin step. Ann got down on her knees and reached her hand into the opening, feeling the ground in all directions. Her arm was in almost up to her elbow when her fingers touched a package of some kind. Ann drew it out. It was a small bundle wrapped roughly in old brown paper.

As Ann turned the package over and began unfolding the paper, she wondered if Andy were playing some kind of last-minute trick. It would be just like him. Then the paper opened and Ann drew in her breath sharply.

There inside lay her diary. Beside it there was a new deerskin cover made to fit over the old brown one. A piece of paper torn off a corner of the wrapping stuck out between the pages of the diary. On it Andy had written in smudged charcoal. "I tuk your diry when I was mad."

So Andy had taken it. And all the time she had been blaming David! As she thought back, she began to understand. Andy had been spying on her when she stamped out his letters, and after she had gone off, he must have come out of hiding and taken the diary from the steps.

Ann fitted the new deerskin cover over the diary. It was very handsome, made from the soft underpart of a deer's skin where the brown shades into a honey color. It looked like a real frontier diary now, Ann thought as she stroked it. She began to turn the pages over, re-reading parts she had written. All at once it struck her that on the inside her diary wasn't much like a frontier diary. For the first time she noticed that she had hardly written anything about the Western Country. Most of her entries were about Gettysburg, about Margaret, about her homesickness. If any outsider were to pick up this diary and read it, he might not even know where it had been written. She turned the pages more slowly. She had never mentioned what Hamilton Hill looked like. Ann jumped up. She didn't want to think about Hamilton Hill now. She didn't care if her diary did have a handsome new cover, she didn't feel one bit like writing in it. She went inside the cabin and put the diary up on her shelf.

All day long as Ann went about her chores,

she felt out-of-sorts and out of courage. It wasn't only that the McPhales had gone East while she was staying behind. She didn't know what was bothering her, but everything she did went wrong. She cut her finger when she was chopping pumpkin for her mother to make a pumpkin pie. She spilled half a pail of milk as she was taking lunch to the men in the field. She caught her dress on a prickly bush and tore it. And every time she picked up the baby, he cried.

"This just isn't your day," her mother said toward the middle of the afternoon. "Why don't you go on down the road and try to find some grapes? You'll like that. But mind you don't go too far."

It certainly wasn't her day, Ann thought crossly as she took an empty pail and went out the cabin door. But when she reached the road, she wondered. Maybe, after all, something might yet turn the day her way. The road seemed to have more magic to it than she had ever known. The sun's rays slanted down on it as though they were lighting up a stage where something important was going to happen. There was a difference in the mood of the road. It wasn't a happy, dancing mood, nor a mysterious, moonlight mood. Today there was a grandness to the road, as though it were a carpet unfurling over the hill before some glorious secret. As Ann stood in the middle of the road, holding her pail in front of her, two golden leaves drifted down, turning slowly over and over in the air, and settled in the bottom of her pail. A wild goose dipped low, honking, from the sky, like a herald sent ahead with news.

Ann walked down the hill, captured by the spell of the road. As she rounded each bend, she found herself half expecting something wonderful to be waiting on the other side. She didn't know what, but something. From time to time she stopped to pick grapes that had survived the storm. On all the hill, the only sounds were the plopping of grapes in her pail and the occasional long honk of a passing goose. Ann followed the road as it wound its way down the hill, turning corner after corner, looking for grapes but secretly hoping for something she couldn't even put into words.

Her pail was almost full when she suddenly noticed where she was. She was almost to the bottom of the hill. Almost to the spot David had pointed out as the site for the first church. She had let the road lead her farther than she had ever gone alone. Instead of something wonderful lying around the next corner of the road, there was probably something dreadful.

And then Ann heard hoofbeats. They were coming from the east—not just one horse but three or four, and they were not far away.

Ann ducked down behind some tall grass by the side of the road and made herself into the smallest ball she could possibly squeeze into, wrapping her arms tightly around her knees. She held her breath as the first horse rounded the bend of the road. She must not move—not even a finger. She kept her eyes on the road, counting the legs of the horses as they came into sight. Now there were two horses . . . three

. . . four. If four men were traveling together from the East to the West at this time of year, they were probably not settlers. They were likely up to no good. They must be the Doane gang that David had warned her about.

All at once Ann began to tremble all over. The first horse had stopped on the road in front of her. Then the other horses came to a stop. As Ann peeped out between the tall grasses, all she could see was a forest of horse legs. From some place way up high above the legs of the first horse came a deep voice. "Little girl," it said, "I wonder if you could tell me what your mother is having for dinner tonight."

The voice didn't sound like the voice of a horse thief. Slowly Ann lifted her eyes from the legs of the horse to the boots of the rider. Slowly she lifted them to the place where the voice had come from. Then she found herself looking into the most wonderful face she had ever seen.

It was a strong face, kind and good, and there was something strangely familiar about it. It was as if Ann ought to know this man, as if she almost knew him. No matter what David had said about strangers, somehow Ann knew deep inside that he hadn't been talking about this one. She stopped feeling afraid. She stood up.

"My mother is having peas and potatoes and corn bread for our evening meal," she said, "and she's baking pumpkin pie."

The man smiled. He leaned down toward Ann. "Would you tell her," he said, "that General George Washington would like to take supper with her?"

For a moment Ann could not believe her ears. General Washington on Hamilton Hill! Then all at once she knew it was true. This was the way she had pictured George Washington from what Arthur Scott had said about him. This must have been just how Washington looked, riding among the men at Valley Forge. Suddenly Arthur Scott's words flashed into her mind. "He always seemed to be there just when our courage began to peter out."

Ann swallowed hard. She tried to drop a

curtsy but it turned out to be just a stiff little bob. She tried to find her voice, but it didn't turn out any better than the curtsy. It was more like a squeak. "My mother will be pleased," she said. "I'll tell her."

Then Ann found herself and her pail of grapes up on the saddle in front of one of the men in General Washington's party. He said he was Dr. Craik, a friend of the General's, but Ann didn't pay much attention. She didn't even look at the other men. All she could see was the white horse in front of her and the straight back of General Washington going up Hamilton Hill. The road itself seemed almost to be moving them up the hill in a kind of magic dream. Except it wasn't a dream, Ann reminded herself. It was true—gloriously, wonderfully true. For some unbelievable reason, General George Washington was on the western side of the mountains and he was going to have supper on Hamilton Hill.

Suddenly Ann turned to Dr. Craik. "Why did General Washington come here?" she asked.

"He owns land in this county," Dr. Craik replied. "He's come to check on it."

"He owns land *here*—in Washington County?" Ann repeated.

Dr. Craik smiled. "Yes, he can't move here, but he bought land because he believes in this part of the country. Some day this land will be worth a great deal of money. He wants to do all he can to develop this side of the mountains."

Ann fell silent, her eyes on General Washington. Again she pictured him at Valley Forge. A lot of people hadn't believed in a free and independent country, she thought. But Washington had. And now he believed in the Western Country. It wasn't just fathers and brothers and settlers who believed in it and owned land here. *George Washington did too*.

Ann and Dr. Craik jogged up the hill. The other men called back and forth to each other, but Ann didn't hear them.

Afterward Ann could never remember just how she introduced General Washington and his friends to her mother. When she caught her breath again, they had started on a tour of the farm with David. Ann and her mother were alone in the cabin with supper to prepare.

Mrs. Hamilton's eyes were shining as she stepped away from the door. "Now is the time to use the linen tablecloth, Ann," she said, "and the lavender flowered plates."

Ann was standing in the doorway, her head in the clouds, watching the men put up their horses. At her mother's words, she came quickly down to the world. What a wonderful world it was, she thought, as she flew over to her mother's chest for the linen tablecloth.

"The food is almost ready," Mrs. Hamilton said. "I'll take care of that while you set the table."

Ann spread out the white linen cloth on the table. She smoothed it gently over the rough boards. She pulled it to hang even on all sides. She unwrapped nine flowered plates and placed them around the table. She put knives, forks, and spoons at each place and set new tall candles in the center of the table.

Then Ann stepped back to look at what she had done. Somehow the whole room seemed changed; it seemed larger and more dignified. The clothes hanging awkwardly on hooks along the wall drew back into the shadows. All the light from the fire and from the open doorway fell on the gleaming white party table, waiting for General Washington.

"It's more beautiful than any table we ever set in Gettysburg," Ann whispered.

Mrs. Hamilton looked up from the hearth and smiled.

Later the table looked even more wonderful, piled high with steaming food—hot yellow corn bread, round bowls of green peas, roasted brown potatoes, a platter of cold venison, bowls of purple grape jelly, golden pumpkin pies. It was the same meal that they had had nearly every evening all summer on Hamilton Hill, but tonight with the lavender flowered plates, it managed to look different.

"I hope I look different too," Ann thought as she fingered her two blue hair ribbons and hastily tied the sash of a fresh apron.

She felt different. General Washington and Mr. Hamilton led the others into the cabin, and suddenly Ann found herself feeling strangely shy. All the time they were taking their places at the table, she kept her eyes down. It was not until her father was asking the blessing that she stole her first look up from under half-closed eyelashes. When she saw George Washington's head bowed over the white tablecloth and lavender plate, the peas and potatoes, Ann thought she could hardly bear her happiness.

During the rest of the meal, Ann followed the conversation in a kind of daze. She didn't seem to hear anything that anyone said, except General Washington. Everything he said rang out clear, with a special meaning, it almost seemed, just for her.

"If I were a young man," General Washington said, "preparing to begin the world, I know of no country where I should rather live."

"I am determined to find a way," he said again, "that we can join the waters of the West with those of the East so that the two countries may be close together."

Ann held onto every word, turned them over in her mind, locked them away in her heart. It was after the evening meal, after all the thank-you's had been said and General Washington and his party were preparing to leave that he said what Ann was to treasure forever afterward. He stood at the doorway, looking toward the west, his eyes resting on Hamilton Hill, yet somehow going beyond.

"The future is traveling west with people like you," he said to Mr. Hamilton. "Here is the rising world—to be kept or lost in the same way a battlefield is kept or lost."

General Washington turned to Ann and put his hand gently on her shoulder. "Through the courage of young girls as much as anyone's. You will live to see this whole country a rolling farmland, bright with houses and barns and churches. Some day. I envy you, Miss Hamilton."

Ann felt her heart turning over within her.

Even after General Washington had gone, she went on standing in the doorway, still feeling his hand on her shoulder. She looked out on Hamilton Hill. It seemed to her she had never seen it so beautiful—the trees more stately, the sky closer. She remembered the tea party she and her mother had had in the woods. The hill had been lovely that day, too. And, of course, the part of the hill that went up and down with the road had always been wonderful.

Ann looked at her vegetable garden laid flat by the storm. It seemed to her that again she could feel the rain beating down on her and her peas. She could feel her own helplessness and despair as the vines broke all around her and she had to fish pods out from the muddy water. Suddenly Ann knew what she had not known before. She had cried during the storm, but it was not really because she hated the Western Country. It was because she loved her vegetable garden.

Other thoughts began crowding in on Ann almost faster than she could take care of them.

Maybe she had begun to love Hamilton Hill too, without even knowing it. Perhaps that was one reason her thoughts had been so mixed up and she hadn't asked if she could go East.

Ann lifted her chin. Well, she was going to plant another vegetable garden in the spring. It was *important* for her to do it. *She* was important to the Western Country. George Washington had said so. And some day, she thought . . .

Ann caught herself and smiled. Here she was thinking "some day" just like the others.

David, coming back from the road and seeing General Washington off, caught Ann's smile.

"Here's something else for you to smile about," he said. He pulled a small packet of letters from his pocket and fingered through them. "Dr. Craik was given these letters at Devore's Ferry to bring on to us. They had been left there about a week ago. There's one for you." He handed Ann an envelope. It was a letter from Margaret.

All the excitement and all the happiness of

the long day seemed to rush into Ann's feet. She took the letter and she ran—not because she wanted to get anywhere, but just because she had to run. Sometimes, Ann had discovered, there is only one thing to do about gladness and that is—to run. Her two brown braids and blue hair ribbons streaming behind her, she ran to the road, to the crest of the hill where on one side the road dropped away to the west and on the other side it dropped away to the east. Here Ann stopped to catch her breath. She sat down on a rock beside the road and slowly slit open the envelope of Margaret's letter. She didn't want to read it too fast. Letters didn't come often and she wanted to make this first reading last as long as she could.

The sun seemed to follow the path of the road as it rolled west to the evening. Ann read about the new teacher in the Gettysburg school, about the frolic at the Gettysburg Hamiltons'. And then she came to the last paragraph.

"This is the big news," Margaret wrote. "At

last I have persuaded Mother and Father to allow me to do what I have wanted to do for so long. They say that in the spring when someone is going over the mountains, I may go along and spend the spring and summer with Uncle John and Aunt Mary. They have no children, and I am sure I could be a help. Just think how close I will be to you! And I will have a little part in the making of the Western Country, after all—even if it is only for one season."

Ann put the letter down in her lap. She wasn't able to find any words to say, even to herself, all that she was feeling. She looked at the road, gathering up the shadows of the evening. Before her in the distant dusk she could just see the outline of the cabin. A thin spiral of smoke climbed up from the chimney and joined a gray cloud in the sky.

"My cup runneth over," Ann whispered to herself.

That night, in the home of a Colonel Cannon several miles west of Hamilton Hill, before he blew out his candle, General George Washington sat down at a table and wrote this in his diary:

"September 18, 1784. Set out with Doctr. Craik for my Land on Miller's Run, crossed the Monongahela at Devore's Ferry . . . bated at one Hamilton's about 4 miles from it, in Washington County, and lodged at Colo. Cannon's."

That night in the cabin on Hamilton Hill, Ann took down from her shelf her deerskin-covered diary. Her heart was too full to write all she wanted. Instead she wrote in big letters across a whole page:

"September 18, 1784.
GEORGE WASHINGTON WAS HERE."

In smaller letters underneath she added:

"Margaret is coming."

Tomorrow she would write more.

A Postscript from the Author

IF YOU look in George Washington's diary, you will find his words exactly as they are in the last chapter. On September 18, 1784, he "bated" or took supper with the Hamiltons.

I don't know if Ann really kept a diary or not. Most of what happened to her in this book is just a story, but some of it is true. There really was an Ann Hamilton; she was my great-great-grandmother. As long as she lived, she told the story to her children and her children's children, about the wonderful evening when George Washington rode up Hamilton Hill.

There was a David and a Daniel, too, and a Mr. and Mrs. Hamilton, an Uncle John, a Margaret, and an Arthur Scott. If you are the kind of reader who likes to know what happens *after* the story ends, I'll tell you that when Ann grew up, she married Arthur Scott. David married his distant cousin, Margaret, and Daniel moved to Kentucky.

Hamilton Hill is known as Ginger Hill now, but grapevines still grow wild by the side of the road. And the little church is really there, just where David pointed out it would be and where he later helped to build it.

Jean Fritz was born in Hangkow, China, and lived there until she was thirteen. She now lives in Dobbs Ferry, New York, with her husband. They have two children.